POLLYANNA

Eleanor H. Porter

Retold by Colleen Reece

Illustrated by
Ken Save

BARBOUR
PUBLISHING, INC.
Uhrichsville, Ohio

ISBN 1-55748-660-3

All Scripture quotations are taken from the Authorized King James Version of the Bible.

Published by Barbour Publishing, Inc.
P.O. Box 719
Uhrichsville, Ohio 44683
http://www.barbourbooks.com

ecpa Member of the
Evangelical Christian
Publishers Association

Printed in the United States of America.

POLLYANNA

"THAT WILL DO"

1
Like a Bombshell

The letter from the West announcing the death of Miss Polly Harrington's brother-in-law hit Beldingsville, Vermont, like a bomb. Miss Polly's lip curled. Just what she should have expected from the poor young minister who stole Jennie away—but to die and leave an eleven-year-old child for someone else to bring up!

Miss Polly hurried into the kitchen. "Nancy."

The cheerful maid-of-two-months looked up from her sinkful of dishes. "Yes, ma'am?" She continued wiping a pitcher.

"Nancy," the stern voice ordered. "I wish you to stop your work and listen when I'm talking to you."

Nancy reddened. "Yes, ma'am. I was only keepin' on because you 'specially told me to hurry with my dishes."

"That will do." The prim lips set in a tight line then unbuttoned enough to say, "Finish your morning work, then clear the little room at the head of the stairs in the attic. Make up the cot, sweep and clean the room. My niece, Miss Pollyanna Whittier is coming to live with me. She is eleven and will sleep in that room."

"A little girl? Oh, won't that be nice!" Nancy thought of the sunshine her own little sisters made in their home.

"Nice?" Miss Polly looked shocked. "I am a good woman, I hope, and will do my duty."

"But of course you want her, your own sister's child," Nancy stared.

"Really, Nancy. Just because I happened to have a sister silly enough to marry and bring unnecessary children into the world already quite full enough, I can't see why I should want to care for them." Her black, silk skirt rustled and she added sharply, "See you clean the corners." She turned to go, looking far older than her forty years because of her tightly pulled-back black hair, elegant but dark clothing, and haughty expression.

Later on that bright, June morning, Nancy slammed

"A LITTLE GIRL? OH, WON'T THAT BE NICE!"

and banged her way through cleaning the little attic room. "I—just—wish—I—could—dig—out—the—corners—of—her—soul," she muttered, jabbing her pointed cleaning stick murderously. "The idea! Sticking that blessed child 'way off up here in this hot little hole with no fire in winter and with all this big house to pick and choose from." She finished, went out with a bang, and defiantly said, "I hope she *did* hear the bang. A pretty place to put a homesick, lonesome child!"

That afternoon, Nancy's indignation spilled over to Old Tom, the gardener. "Mr. Tom, did you know a little girl's comin' here to live? It's Miss Polly's niece."

A tender light crept into the faded eyes. "Why, it must be Miss Jennie's little gal. Glory-be-to-praise! To think of my old eyes seein' this."

"Who was Miss Jennie?"

"An angel straight from heaven." Old Tom straightened. "She married a minister feller at twenty, and her family never forgave her, even when she named her last

A TENDER LIGHT CREPT INTO THE FADED EYES

baby—all the others died, I heard—after Miss Polly and Miss Anna."

"She's goin' to sleep in the attic."

The old man laughed. "I'm afraid you ain't fond of Miss Polly."

"Who could be?" Nancy retorted.

"You must not know about her love affair. The feller's livin' right in this town but it ain't fit that I should name him." A remembering look came into his lined face. "Miss Polly used to be right handsome and still could, if she'd let herself be. If she'd let that tight hair loose and wear the sort of bonnets with posies and the lacy, white things she used to wear, you'd see." He sighed. "Seems as if she's been feedin' on thistles ever since the trouble, all bitter and prickly."

"There's no pleasin' her," Nancy declared. "I wouldn't stay a minute if the folks at home weren't for needin' my wages. Someday I'll just explode, and it will be goodbye to me."

"SOMEDAY, I'LL JUST EXPLODE"

POLLYANNA

"Nancy," Miss Polly's sharp voice called.

"Yes, ma'am." Nancy scuttled toward the house.

In due time came the telegram saying Pollyanna would reach Beldingsville the next day at four o'clock, the twenty-fifth of June. Miss Polly read the message, frowned and climbed to the attic room. A small, neatly made bed, two straight-backed chairs, a washstand, bureau without mirror, and table made up the furniture. No curtains hung at the dormer windows. No pictures hung on the walls. All day the sun had poured on the roof; the little room resembled an oven. As there were no screens, the windows had stayed closed. A big fly angrily buzzed, trying to get out. Miss Polly killed it, frowned again, and went to find her maid.

"Nancy, I have ordered screens, but until they come, don't open the windows in Miss Pollyanna's room. I found a nasty fly. Now, my niece arrives tomorrow at four. Timothy is to take the open buggy and drive you to the train station. The telegram says Miss Pollyanna has

"MY NIECE ARRIVES TOMORROW AT FOUR"

'light hair, red-checked gingham dress, and straw hat.'"

Nancy started to speak, but Miss Polly added, "I shall not go," and swept from the kitchen.

The next afternoon, good-natured, good-looking Timothy, Old Tom's son, and Nancy, who had already become good friends with him, drove off to get Pollyanna. "I hope for her sake, she's quiet and doesn't drop knives or bang doors," she said while waiting.

"If she ain't, nobody knows what'll become of the rest of us." Timothy grinned. "Imagine Miss Polly and a noisy child. Whew! Say, there goes the whistle."

Soon Nancy saw her, a slender little girl in red-checked gingham. Two fat braids of flaxen hair hung down her back. An eager, freckled face turned right and left beneath a straw hat.

"Are you Miss—Pollyanna?" Nancy faltered when she got courage to go to her. The next minute, two arms half-smothered her.

"Oh, I'm so glad, *glad*, GLAD to see you! I hoped

A SLENDER LITTLE GIRL IN RED-CHECKED GINGHAM

you'd come to meet me. I've been wondering all the way here what you looked like. I'm glad you look just as you do."

"This is Timothy," Nancy stammered. "Maybe you have a trunk?"

"A brand new one," Pollyanna said importantly. "The Ladies' Aid bought it for me. Wasn't it lovely when they wanted a red carpet so? I don't know how much red carpet a trunk could buy, half an aisle, do you think? Oh, Mr. Gray, Mrs. Gray's husband—they're cousins of Deacon Carr's wife and brought me East, said to give you this check so I could get my trunk." She took it from her bag.

Nancy took a long breath. After that speech, she needed one, and all the time Timothy retrieved the trunk and got Pollyanna into the buggy between him and Nancy, the visitor kept up a steady stream of questions.

"I love to ride." Pollyanna bounced a bit. "What a pretty street. Father said it would be—" She choked. "Mrs. Gray told me to explain about the red gingham

"WHAT A PRETTY STREET"

dress. There weren't any black things in the last missionary barrel but a worn, velvet basque, not at all suitable. It would be harder to be glad in black—"

"Glad!" Nancy gasped.

"Yes, that Father's gone to Heaven to be with Mother and the rest. I wanted him to stay 'cause I only had the Ladies' Aid, but now I have you, Aunt Polly."

"Oh, you've made an awful mistake! I ain't your Aunt Polly. I'm Nancy, the hired girl." She ignored Timothy's chuckle.

"But there *is* an Aunt Polly, isn't there?" Pollyanna demanded. When Timothy said, "You bet your life there is," the child brightened. "Then I'm glad she didn't come to meet me. Now I have you, and her still coming. Father said she lived in a lovely great, big house on a hill."

"It's the white one with green blinds up ahead."

"I've never seen such a lot of trees and green grass." Pollyanna stared. "Nancy, is my Aunt Polly rich?"

"Yes, miss."

"I'M NANCY, THE HIRED GIRL"

POLLYANNA

"It must be perfectly lovely to have lots of money. I never knew anyone that did, only the Whites—they're some rich. They have carpets in every room and ice cream Sundays. Does Aunt Polly have ice-cream Sundays?"

Nancy shook her head. "No, Miss. I guess she doesn't like ice cream. I never saw it on her table."

"Doesn't she? Anyhow, I can be glad 'cause the ice cream you don't eat can't make your stomach ache. Does Aunt Polly have carpets in every room?"

The maid scowled, thinking of the bare floor in the attic room. "Well, in 'most every room."

"I love carpet," Pollyanna confided. "We just had two little ones from the missionary barrel and one had ink spots." She chattered happily on, exclaiming over the beautiful house.

While Timothy unloaded the trunk, he told Nancy, "It'll be more fun here now, with that kid around, than movin'-picture shows every day."

"I guess it'll not be so fun for that blessed child. She'll

"IT'LL BE MORE FUN HERE NOW, WITH THAT KID AROUND"

need a rock to fly to for refuge. I'm a-goin' to be that rock!" She turned and led Pollyanna up the steps.

Inside, Pollyanna flew across the room and into her aunt's scandalized, unyielding lap. "It's so lovely to have you and Nancy after just having the Ladies' Aid!"

Miss Polly held her off and cut short her explanation about the red gingham dress and added, "I don't care to have you talk about your father." She rose and took Pollyanna upstairs, over thick carpet and past gorgeous rooms.

"How awfully glad you must be to be rich."

"Poll*anna*, I hope I will never be sinfully proud of riches," Miss Polly said and opened the door of the attic room, which she'd chosen to get the child as far from her own rooms as possible. With a few words, she left her in the barren, ugly room.

Nancy found Pollyanna on her knees a few minutes later. "I can be glad there's no looking glass 'cause I can't see my freckles," the child said. She looked out the

"I HOPE I WILL NEVER BE SINFULLY PROUD OF RICHES"

window to the silvery river and church spire. "And I don't need pictures. I'm glad to be here." Nancy hurried out to hide her anger and Pollyanna threw open the windows, then stepped into the branches of a great tree and swung down.

POLLYANNA STEPPED INTO THE BRANCHES OF A GREAT TREE

A SLENDER, WINDBLOWN FIGURE STOOD ON A HUGE ROCK

2
Pollyanna's Glad Game

Nancy rushed into the garden. "Mr. Tom, Mr. Tom, that blessed child's gone right up into Heaven, poor lamb, and me told to give her bread and milk in the kitchen 'cause she didn't come down to dinner and she ain't in her room!"

"Heaven?" The old man looked into the brilliant sunset sky and pointed. A slender, windblown figure stood on a huge rock in the distance. "It does look as if she tried to get as nigh Heaven as she could."

"For the land's sakes, Miss Pollyanna, what a scare you give me!" Panting from her run, Nancy met Pollyanna and hurried her toward home. "I guess you flew right up through the roof."

Pollyanna skipped gleefully. "I flew down instead of up. I came down the tree outside my window."

"My stars and stockings!" Nancy shrieked. "Don't tell your aunt! Hurry! I've got to get my dishes done.

You'll have to have bread and milk in the kitchen with me. I'm sorry. Your aunt didn't like your not comin' down to dinner."

"I'm not. I'm glad." Pollyanna laughed merrily. "I like bread and milk, and I'd like to eat with you. I don't see any trouble about being glad about that."

"You don't seem to see any trouble bein' glad about anything." Nancy remembered Pollyanna's brave attempts to like the bare little attic room.

"Well, that's the game. Father told it to me, and it's lovely. We've played it since I was a little, little girl. Some of the Ladies' Aid played it, too."

"Game? I ain't much on games," Nancy said doubtfully.

"We began when some crutches came in the missionary barrel," Pollyanna explained, face aglow.

"*Crutches?*"

"Yes. I wanted a doll and Father had written them so, but when the barrel came, the lady wrote there weren't

"I AIN'T MUCH ON GAMES"

any dolls, but maybe some child could use the crutches."

"I don't see any game about that," Nancy said crossly.

"The game was to find something to be glad about. I couldn't see it, either," she added honestly. "I cried. Then Father said we could be glad, *glad*, GLAD that we *didn't need the crutches*."

"Well, I never." Nancy threw up her hands.

"We've played it ever since. The harder 'tis, the more fun 'tis, except sometimes it's almost too hard, like when Father went to Heaven."

"Or when you're stuck in a snippy little room."

Pollyanna sighed. "That was hard, at first, 'specially when I felt so lonesome and had been wanting pretty things. I wonder if Aunt Polly would play."

Nancy groaned and quickly said, "I ain't sayin' I can play it very well, but I'll play with you."

Pollyanna gave her a rapturous hug. "That will be splendid. We'll have so much fun."

After Pollyanna finished her bread and milk, she went

"WE'LL HAVE SO MUCH FUN"

into the sitting room where her aunt sat reading.

"I'm sorry to have been obliged so soon to send you to the kitchen to eat bread and milk," she said.

"I was real glad," the little girl told her. "You mustn't feel bad one bit."

Aunt Polly sat up straighter. "It's high time you were in bed. Nancy will give you a candle. Breakfast will be at half-past seven."

Pollyanna came straight to her and gave her a hug. "I've had a beautiful time so far," she said. "I know I'm going to love living with you." She ran happily out.

"What an extraordinary child," Miss Polly gasped. "She's 'glad' I punished her, and I 'mustn't feel bad one bit' and she's going to 'love living with me.' Well, upon my soul!"

Fifteen minutes later in the attic room, a lonely little girl sobbed, "I know, Father-among-the-angels, I'm not playing the game one bit now, but I don't believe even you could find anything to be glad about sleeping all alone

"WHAT AN EXTRAORDINARY CHILD"

'way off up here in the dark."

Downstairs, Nancy jabbed her dish-mop into the milk pitcher and muttered jerkily, "If playin' a silly-fool game about bein' glad you've got crutches when you want dolls is got to be my way of bein' that rock of refuge, why, I'm a-goin' to play it, I am, I am!"

Shortly after seven the next morning, Pollyanna pelted down the stairs, into the garden and flung her arms around Miss Polly. "I saw you from my window and you looked so good, I just had to come down and hug you."

Her aunt stammered and walked rapidly away.

"Do you always work in the garden, Mr. Man?" Pollyanna asked the gardener.

"Yes. I'm Old Tom. You're so like your mother—"

The breakfast bell and Nancy flying out the door cut short their conversation. "Always run when you hear the bell," she told the little girl.

At breakfast, two flies sailed over the table. "Nancy," said Miss Polly sternly. "Where did those flies come from?"

"DO YOU ALWAYS WORK IN THE GARDEN, MR. MAN?"

POLLYANNA

"I reckon maybe they're my flies," Pollyanna said innocently. "There were lots of them upstairs this morning."

"Yours? What do you mean? Pollyanna, did you raise those windows that don't have screens?"

"W-hy, yes."

"Nancy," Miss Polly ordered. "Go shut those windows immediately and the doors. Then kill every fly you find. As for you, Pollyanna, you've forgotten your duty. I know it's warm but it's your duty to keep those windows closed until the screens come." After breakfast she gave her niece a little pamphlet on flies. Pollyanna immediately took it, read it, and came back with sparkling face to thank Aunt Polly for the interesting reading material!

Every time Polly Harrington attempted to guide her newly acquired niece, she ran into all kinds of things. Pollyanna wanted to know if her aunt had ever received a missionary barrel. She brought out her scant wardrobe for examination, and Miss Polly shuddered. Pollyanna didn't

"W-HY, YES"

act interested in music, had little skill in sewing, and the extent of her cooking was chocolate fudge and fig cake. When her aunt lined out a busy program, she cried out in dismay, "You haven't left me any time just to live! To play outdoors and read to myself: to climb hills and talk to Mr. Tom and Nancy and find out about the houses and people."

"If I'm willing to do my duty by you, it seems you should be able to do yours and not act ungrateful." Miss Polly stood to end the interview.

"Why, I love you, Aunt Polly! I couldn't be ungrateful. But," she said wistfully, "isn't there any way you can be glad about this duty business?"

Red-cheeked and angry, Polly Harrington said, "Don't be impertinent!" And swept down the stairs.

In the hot little attic room Pollyanna sighed. "I didn't mean to be impertinent," she whispered. "I guess I can be glad when the duty's done."

Shopping with Pollyanna exhausted her aunt and took

"DON'T BE IMPERTINENT!"

up the whole afternoon. Pollyanna came from it smiling and happy for as she told a clerk, to her aunt's extreme embarrassment, "When you haven't had anybody but missionary barrels and Ladies' Aiders to dress you, it's perfectly lovely to just walk in and buy clothes that are brand-new and don't have to be tucked up or let down."

After supper Pollyanna learned more of her mother from Old Tom and of Nancy's family on the little farm six miles away.

"They have lovely names," Nancy said. "I just hate being Nancy."

"You can be glad it isn't Hephzibah, like Mrs. White," Pollyanna told her, and Nancy giggled in spite of herself when the little girl added, "Her husband always called out 'Hep, Hep,' and she said she thought he'd add, 'and Hurrah!'"

Hot and miserable that night, Pollyanna caught up a long white bag containing Miss Polly's sealskin coat for a bed, others for sheet and pillow. She stuffed them out

"I JUST HATE BEING NANCY"

the window to the roof below her aunt's sun parlor. Closing the window behind her, she quickly fell asleep in the cool air, after walking back and forth to hear the tin roof crackle.

Aunt Polly heard the noise and phoned for Timothy. "Someone is on the roof of the sun parlor. Come quick! He can get into the house through the attic window."

Pollyanna awakened to see a lantern flash and a trio of startled faces: Timothy stood on top of a ladder, Old Tom was just getting through the window, and Aunt Polly peered out at her from behind him. "Pollyanna, what does this mean?" her aunt cried.

She blinked and sat up. "Why, don't look so scared! It isn't that I've got consumption and have to sleep outdoors. It's just I got so hot in there. I shut the windows, Aunt Polly, so the flies couldn't carry the germs in."

Her aunt didn't reply until the men had gone. Then she said sternly, "Hand me those things at once and come in here."

"COME QUICK!"

POLLYANNA

Pollyanna could barely breathe inside the stifling room after the outside coolness. At the top of the stairs, Miss Polly jerked out crisply, "You'll sleep with me for the rest of the night. The screens will be here tomorrow. Until then it's my duty to know where you are!"

"With you—in your bed?" she cried rapturously. "Oh, Aunt Polly, how perfectly lovely of you! And when I've so wanted to sleep with someone sometime that belonged to me, not just a Ladies' Aider. My! I reckon I am glad those screens didn't come. Wouldn't you be?"

Miss Polly didn't reply but stalked on ahead, feeling curiously helpless. For the third time since Pollyanna's arrival, Miss Polly had been forced to punish her niece. And for the third time, she had to face the amazing fact that Pollyanna saw her punishment as a special reward of merit. No wonder Miss Polly felt curiously helpless.

NO WONDER MISS POLLY FELT CURIOUSLY HELPLESS

SHE FREQUENTLY MET THE MAN

3
Going Visiting

Life at the Harrington homestead settled into something like order—though not exactly the order Miss Polly had first prescribed. Pollyanna sewed, practiced on the piano, read aloud, and studied cooking in the kitchen but didn't give any of those things the time originally planned. Every afternoon from two until six was hers to "just live," as she said. It offered time for her to do pretty much as she liked—as long as things weren't prohibited by her aunt—and time for Aunt Polly to be away from the niece who made her exclaim many times, "What an extraordinary child!"

Pleasant afternoons found Pollyanna begging for an errand to run "so she might be off and see people." On her walks, she frequently met "The Man," as she called him.

Unlike other men she met, The Man wore a long black coat. A high, silk hat sat above his clean-shaven, pale face and silver-gray hair showed beneath the hat. Pollyanna felt sorry for The Man who always walked alone. One day she said cheerily, "How do you do, sir? Isn't this a nice day?"

The Man glanced around, then stopped uncertainly. "Did you speak to me?"

"Yes, sir," beamed Pollyanna. "It's a nice day, isn't it?"

"Eh? Oh! Humph!" He grunted and strode off.

What a funny man, Pollyanna thought.

The third time she saw and spoke to him, The Man said, "See here, child, who are you, and why do you speak to me every day?"

"I'm Pollyanna Whittier, and I thought you looked lonesome. Now that we're introduced, only I don't know your name—"

"Well, of all the—" He broke off and walked away faster than ever.

Pollyanna's lips drooped disappointedly, and she went

"SEE HERE, CHILD, WHO ARE YOU...?"

on her way, carrying calf's-foot jelly to Mrs. Snow. Miss Polly felt it a duty to send something once a week to the poor, sick woman, a member of her church. Usually Nancy took the offering but today Pollyanna had begged to do it.

"It's glad I am to get rid of the duty," Nancy rejoiced. "Though it's a shame to be tuckin' the job off onto you, poor lamb."

"But I'd love to do it, Nancy."

"You won't after you've done it once," Nancy said sourly. "She's so cantankerous, a soul wouldn't go near her from mornin' till night if folks weren't sorry for her. I pity her daughter, what has to take care of her. Nothin' ever happens that Mis' Snow thinks is right. If it's Monday she's bound to say she wished 'twas Sunday. If you take her jelly she'll wish 'twas chicken, but if you *did* bring her chicken, she'd be hankerin' for lamb broth!"

"What a funny woman," Pollyanna laughed. "She must be surprising and—and different. I love *different* folks."

"SHE'S SO CANTANKEROUS"

"Well," Nancy sniffed. "Mis' Snow's 'different,' all right—I hope, for the sake of the rest of us."

Now Pollyanna knocked at the gate of the shabby little cottage. A pale-faced, tired-looking young girl answered.

"How do you do?" Pollyanna politely began. "I'm from Miss Polly Harrington and I'd like to see Mrs. Snow, please."

"If you would, you're the first one that ever 'liked' to see her," the girl muttered under her breath, but Pollyanna didn't hear.

In the sickroom, after the girl ushered her in and closed the door, Pollyanna blinked in the gloom, then saw a woman half-sitting up in bed across the room. "How do you do, Mrs. Snow. Aunt Polly says she hopes you are comfortable today, and she sent you some calf's-foot jelly."

"Dear me! Jelly?" murmured a fretful voice. "Of course, I'm obliged but I was hoping 'twould be lamb broth today."

"HOW DO YOU DO, MRS. SNOW"

POLLYANNA

Pollyanna frowned a little. "Why, I thought it was *chicken* you wanted when folks brought you jelly. Nancy said so, and 'twas lamb broth when we brought chicken, but maybe 'twas the other way around."

The sick woman pulled herself up until she sat erect, a most unusual thing, though Pollyanna didn't know this. "Well, Miss Impertinence, who are you?" she demanded.

Pollyanna laughed gleefully. "Oh, *that* isn't my name—and I'm so glad, too. That would be worse than Hephzibah, wouldn't it? I'm Pollyanna Whittier, Miss Polly Harrington's niece, and I've come to live with her. That's why I'm here with the jelly."

The woman fell back on her pillow. "Very well; thank you. My appetite isn't very good this morning. I didn't sleep a wink last night."

"I wish *I* hadn't." Pollyanna placed the jelly on a little stand and settled into the nearest chair. "You lose so much time just sleeping. You might be just living, you know. It seems a pity we can't live nights, too."

"I DIDN'T SLEEP A WINK LAST NIGHT"

POLLYANNA

Again the sick woman pulled herself up. "Well, if you ain't the amazing young one," she cried. "Pull up the window curtain. I should like to know what you look like."

Pollyanna rose, but laughed ruefully. "O dear! Then you'll see my freckles, just when I was being so glad it was dark, and you couldn't see them." She raised the curtain and turned back to the bed, excitedly saying, "Now I can see you. They didn't tell me you were so pretty."

"Me—pretty?" the woman scoffed bitterly. Mrs. Snow had lived forty years and been too busy for fifteen of them wishing things were different to find time to enjoy things as they were.

"Oh, but your eyes are big and dark, and your hair's all black and curly. I love black curls. (That's one of the things I'm going to have when I get to Heaven.) You've got two little red spots in your cheeks. Why, Mrs. Snow, you are pretty. I should think you'd know when you looked in the glass."

"THEY DIDN'T TELL ME YOU WERE SO PRETTY"

POLLYANNA

"If you laid flat on your back as I am you wouldn't be doing much primping before the mirror, either."

Pollyanna skipped to get a mirror then stopped. "May I fix your hair first, please?"

"Why, I s'pose so," Mrs. Snow said grudgingly. "But it won't stay, you know."

Five minutes later, Pollyanna laid the comb down that had fluffed the black curls, plumped the pillow and tucked a pink flower into Mrs. Snow's hair. "I like red flowers better," she complained but still stared at her reflection.

"It's kind of hard to be glad about things when you're lying in bed," Polly sympathized. "I'll think and think and tell you next time I come." She tripped out the doorway, leaving Mrs. Snow wondering, and her daughter Milly staring when she came in to find the curtain up, her mother wearing a flower in her hair and complaining, "I should think *somebody* might give me a new nightdress—instead of lamb broth."

"I LIKE RED FLOWERS BETTER"

"Why, Mother!" No wonder Milly gasped. Two new nightdresses she'd been begging her mother to wear for months lay in the bureau drawer behind her.

After several more days of Pollyanna's speaking to The Man and getting grunts, he scowled and told her: "I have something to think of besides the weather. I don't know whether the sun shines or not."

Pollyanna beamed joyously. "I thought you didn't. That's why I told you, so you'd notice when the sun shines."

He looked startled. "Why don't you find someone your own age to talk to?"

"There aren't any 'round here, Nancy says. I don't mind. I like old folks just as well—being used to the Ladies' Aid."

"Ladies' Aid indeed! Is that what you took me for?" He almost smiled.

"You don't look a mite like a Ladies' Aider, and I'm sure you're much nicer than you look!"

THE MAN MADE A FUNNY NOISE IN HIS THROAT

POLLYANNA

The Man made a funny noise in his throat and marched off, but the next time he saw her, he actually smiled, and from then on, spoke to her.

"Sakes alive, Miss Pollyanna," Nancy gasped one day when this happened. "Did that man *speak to you*?"

"He always does now."

"But he never speaks to anyone, not for years. He's John Pendleton and lives in the big house on Pendleton Hill. He won't even have anyone 'round to cook for him—comes down to the hotel for his meals. Sally Miner, who waits on him, says he hardly opens his head enough to say what he wants to eat. She has to guess—only it will be *cheap*. He ain't poor. He's got loads of money, but he's savin' it."

"How splendid," Pollyanna cried. "For the heathen. That's denying yourself and taking up your cross. Father told me."

"Some say he's got a skeleton in his closet and is crazy. Others say he's just cross."

"DID THAT MAN SPEAK TO YOU?"

Pollyanna shuddered. "Why doesn't he throw it away?"

Nancy chuckled and told how John Pendleton traveled a lot in heathen countries. Pollyanna decided he must be a missionary and added how glad she was he spoke to her.

The next time she visited Mrs. Snow, the fretful woman said she'd wanted Pollyanna to come the day before. Pollyanna raised the shade and said, "Now, just see what I brought."

"What is it?" Mrs. Snow looked at the basket.

"What do you want?"

"Nothing, really. Of course, there's lamb broth—"

"I've got it," crowed Pollyanna.

"That's what I *didn't* want," sighed the sick woman. "It was chicken I wanted."

"I've got that, too." Pollyanna chuckled. "And calf's-foot jelly." She arranged the three dishes. "How do you do today?"

"Very poorly. Nellie Higgins next door was practicing music, and I lost my nap."

"I'VE GOT THAT, TOO"

Pollyanna clapped her hands. "I promised you I'd find something for you to be glad about. I thought—how glad you can be—that other folks aren't sick like you."

Mrs. Snow stared angrily but Pollyanna rushed on. "Now I'll tell you about the game." She began the story of the missionary barrel, the crutches, and the doll that didn't come. After Nancy came for Pollyanna, Milly saw tears on her mother's cheeks.

The July days passed. A few times Pollyanna tried to mention the game to her aunt, but as it required talking about her father, she broke off. One afternoon she met Miss Polly on the stairs to her little room. "Come right in," she invited. "I love company." She chattered away but bit her lip when she betrayed how much she'd planned on having lace curtains and pretty carpets.

Miss Polly rose, face red. "That will do, Pollyanna." She swept down the stairs. A little later she directed Nancy to move Pollyanna's belongings to a beautiful room below, with carpets and pictures. Nancy said, "O glory!" to herself and hurried to obey.

NANCY HURRIED TO OBEY

... A FORLORN GRAY BUNCH OF NEGLECTED MISERY

4
A Kitten, A Dog—and Jimmy Bean

August came, bringing surprises—none of which shocked Nancy, who expected surprises since Pollyanna arrived.

First, the kitten. Pollyanna found it pitifully mewing down the road. No one claimed it, so she brought home the forlorn gray bunch of neglected misery, covered with mange and fleas. "I'm glad I couldn't find who owned it," she confided. "I love kitties and I knew you'd be glad to let it live here."

Miss Polly hated cats, especially sick, mangy, flea-covered cats. She opened her lips to tell her niece to get rid of the beast but found no words after Pollyanna said, "I told Mrs. Ford you wouldn't let a dear little kitty go hunting for a home when you'd just taken *me* in." Before her aunt could speak, Pollyanna ran to Nancy, calling, "Aunt Polly is going to bring this dear little kitty up along with me!"

POLLYANNA

The next day it was a dog, even dirtier and more forlorn. Again, Polly Harrington found herself figuring as a kind protector and angel of mercy, a role thrust upon her by Pollyanna. She hated dogs even more than cats but found herself powerless to turn it away, so said nothing.

However, when in less than a week Pollyanna brought home a small, ragged boy and confidently claimed the same protection for him, Miss Polly did have something to say.

On a pleasant Thursday morning, Pollyanna had been taking calf's-foot jelly again to Mrs. Snow, who had begun playing the game, in spite of many mistakes. A boy sat in a little heap by the roadside, whittling on a small stick.

"Hullo," Pollyanna said and smiled.

"Hullo yourself," he mumbled.

"My name's Pollyanna Whittier," she said. "What's yours?"

"Jimmy Bean," he grunted.

"JIMMY BEAN"

"Good. Now we're introduced. I live at Miss Polly Harrington's house. Where do you live?"

"Nowhere. I'm ten years old, goin' on eleven. I come last year to live at the Orphan's Home; but they've got so many kids, there ain't much room for me an' I wasn't never wanted, anyhow, I don't believe. So I quit. I'd like a home with a mother instead of a Matron. I hain't had folks since Dad died. I've tried four houses but they didn't want me, though I said I expected to work. There! Is that all you want to know?" His voice broke on the last sentences.

"Why, what a shame!" Pollyanna sympathized. "I know just how you feel because after my father died, there wasn't anybody but the Ladies' Aid for me until Aunt Polly said she'd take—" Pollyanna stopped abruptly. A wonderful idea began to show in her face.

"Oh, I know just the place for you," she cried. "Aunt Polly'll take you—I know she will! Didn't she take me? And Fluffy and Buffy, and they're only a cat and a dog.

"AUNT POLLY'LL TAKE YOU—I KNOW SHE WILL!"

Come, you don't know how good and kind Aunt Polly is."

Jimmy Bean's thin little face brightened. "Honest Injun? I'd work, you know, and I'm real strong!" He bared a small, bony arm."

"Of course she would. It's an awful big house. Maybe you'll have to sleep in the attic room at first. I did. You've got freckles, too, so you'll be glad there isn't any looking glass, and the outdoor picture is nicer than any wall-one could be," panted Pollyanna.

They reached the house, and she piloted her companion straight to her aunt. "Oh, Aunt Polly," she triumphed. "Just look a-here! I've got something ever so much nicer than Fluffy and Buffy for you to bring up. It's a real live boy, and he won't mind a bit sleeping in the attic, and he says he'll work; but I shall need him to play with."

Miss Polly grew white then very red. "Pollyanna, what does this mean? Where did you find this dirty little boy?"

The "dirty little boy" stepped back and looked at the door. Pollyanna laughed merrily. "I reckon he'll improve

"WHERE DID YOU FIND THIS DIRTY LITTLE BOY?"

by washing, just like Fluffy and Buffy. This is Jimmy Bean, and I brought him here to live with you. He wants a home and folks."

"That will do, Pollyanna. As if a tramp cat and a mangy dog weren't bad enough. Now you must needs bring home a ragged little beggar from the street, who—"

Jimmy Bean's eyes flashed. His chin came up. He walked straight to Miss Polly. "I ain't a beggar, marm, an' I don't want nothin' of you. I wouldn't have come to your old house if she hadn't made me, a-tellin' me you was so good and kind that you'd just be dyin' to take me in. So there!" He stalked out.

"Oh, Aunt Polly," choked Pollyanna. "I thought you'd be *glad* to have him here!"

Miss Polly raised her hand for silence, the boy's scornful, "good and kind" ringing in her ears. "Pollyanna," she cried sharply. "*Will* you stop using that everlasting word 'glad'! It's 'glad,' 'glad,' 'glad' from morning till night until I think I shall grow wild!"

"I AIN'T A BEGGAR, MARM"

Pollyanna's jaw dropped from sheer amazement and she hurried blindly from the room and outdoors after Jimmy Bean. She found him at the end of the driveway. "I want you to know how sorry I am," she panted.

"I ain't blamin' you," retorted the boy, sullenly. "But I ain't no beggar!"

"Of course you aren't. I probably didn't explain it right. I wish I could find a place for you." Her face lighted. "Say, the Ladies' Aid meets this afternoon. I'll lay your case before them. That's what Father always did when he wanted anything—educating the heathen and new carpets."

The boy turned fiercely. "I ain't a heathen or a new carpet. Besides, what's a Ladies' Aid?"

Pollyanna looked horrified that he didn't know. "It's a lot of ladies that meet and sew, and they're awfully kind. I'm going to tell them about you this afternoon."

"Not much you won't! Stand around and hear a whole lot of women call me a beggar instead of just one? Not much!"

"I'LL LAY YOUR CASE BEFORE THEM"

"I'll go alone," she quickly promised.

"Don't forget to say I'd work."

"Of course not. I'll let you know tomorrow by the road where I found you today, near Mrs. Snow's house."

"I'll be there. Maybe I'll go back to the Home tonight, even though they ain't like *folks*. They don't *care*."

Miss Polly, who had been watching from the window, sighed and turned away—feeling somehow she had lost something important.

Miss Polly didn't attend the Ladies' Aid meeting that afternoon, and her niece rejoiced. Mrs. Ford, the minister's wife, asked if her aunt had sent her.

"Oh, no," she quickly replied. "I've come to lay a case before you. Jimmy Bean is ten going on eleven and wants a home with a mother instead of a Matron. I thought some of you might like him to live with you." She paused. "I forgot to say he will work."

A few of the women coldly questioned her, then talked among themselves. Pollyanna listened with growing

"I THOUGHT SOME OF YOU MIGHT LIKE HIM TO LIVE WITH YOU"

concern and her heart sank. Not one woman there would take Jimmy. Mrs. Ford suggested that instead of sending so much money to the little boys in far-away India they might assume the support of Jimmy, but the women protested.

"We're known for our offering to Hindu missions," they said. "Why, we'd be mortified if it is less this year."

"Not but that it's good to send money to the heathen," Pollyanna sighed as she sorrowfully trudged along. "But they acted as if the little boys *here* weren't of any account." Unwilling to go home, she headed for Pendleton Hill. A dog she had once seen with The Man, Mr. John Pendleton, ran toward her barking, then raced back and forth in the path. Pollyanna followed. She soon found John Pendleton lying motionless at the foot of a steep, overhanging mass of rock.

"I've hurt my leg," he told her. "My house is about five minutes' walk from here." He brought out keys and singled out one. "Go in the side door. You'll find a

"I'VE HURT MY LEG"

telephone. Dr. Thomas Chilton's number is on a card. Tell the doctor John Pendleton is at the foot of Little Eagle Ledge in Pendleton Woods with a broken leg. He'll know what to do."

Pollyanna hurried to do his bidding. Before long, she saw the great pile of gray stone with pillared verandas, a little frightening. Inside the somber house, she found the telephone and made the call, then ran back to the injured man. "The doctor is coming as soon as he can. I came back to be with you. You're only cross *outside*, you aren't cross inside." She pointed to the dog lying under his master's hand. "Dogs and cats know how folks are inside better than other folks do." She got the man's head into her lap and stroked it.

"Well, little lady, playing nurse?" kind-eyed Dr. Chilton asked when he arrived.

"Oh, no, but I'm glad I was here." The doctor nodded and said, "So am I," then set about his work.

The next afternoon, Pollyanna told the disappointed

"WELL, LITTLE LADY, PLAYING NURSE?"

Jimmy Bean about her Ladies' Aid meeting but promised to write to her own Ladies' Aid out West to see if someone would take him. Jimmy brightened and reminded her to say he'd work.

About a week later, Pollyanna asked if she could take Mrs. Snow's calf's-foot jelly to Mr. Pendleton instead, because of his broken leg.

"*John Pendleton!* I do not care to send jelly to him." Miss Polly added curiously, "Does he know who you are and where you live, that I am your aunt?"

"I reckon not. I told him my name once, but he never calls me by it." She shifted impatiently from one foot to the other.

"Very well," Aunt Polly said at last, in a strange-sounding voice so unlike her own. "You may take the jelly, but be sure he understands that it is your gift, and that I did not send it."

"Yes'm—no'm—thank you, Aunt Polly," exulted Pollyanna as she flew through the door.

"I DO NOT CARE TO SEND JELLY TO HIM"

"MAYBE YOU'D LIKE TO SEE OUR PATIENT, EH?"

5
Just Like a Book

The great gray pile of stone looked very different when Pollyanna visited John Pendleton the second time. Windows stood open, an elderly woman was hanging out clothes in the back yard and the doctor's gig sat outside.

A familiar-looking small dog bounded to meet her, and the woman left her duty to open the door.

"I've brought some calf's-foot jelly for Mr. Pendleton." Pollyanna smiled.

"Thank you." The woman reached for the bowl.

Dr. Chilton stepped into the hall just then. "Calf's-foot jelly. That will be fine. Maybe you'd like to see our patient, eh?"

"Oh, yes, sir." Pollyanna beamed and trotted down the hall.

"But Doctor, didn't Mr. Pendleton give orders not to admit anyone?"

"Yes, but I'm giving orders now. This little girl is better than a six-quart bottle of tonic any day. If anybody can take the grouch out of Pendleton, she can."

"Indeed!" The man nurse from the city smiled. "What are the special ingredients of this wonder-working— tonic?"

The doctor shook his head. "Just being glad, according to my other patients. I don't know her well yet, but I already wish I could prescribe her the way I do pills. We'd be out of nursing and doctoring soon!"

Pollyanna, unaware of Dr. Chilton's discussion, walked through the great library and into a nearby room where a very cross-looking man lay in bed. "See here, didn't I say— oh, it's you."

"I brought you some calf's-foot jelly. I hope you like it."

"Never ate it." He scowled.

Disappointment came into his visitor's face. "Then you can't know that you *don't* like it, can you? You can

"I ALREADY WISH I COULD PRESCRIBE HER THE WAY I DO PILLS"

be glad about that. Now if you knew—"

"I know I'm flat on my back and liable to stay here till doomsday, I guess."

Pollyanna looked shocked. "It couldn't be till doomsday, when the angel Gabriel blows his trumpet, unless it comes quicker—the Bible says it may, but I—"

John Pendleton suddenly laughed.

"Broken legs don't last, like lifelong invalids same as Mrs. Snow. You can be glad you just broke one and 'twasn't two."

He raised his eyebrows. "I suppose I might be glad I wasn't a centipede and didn't break fifty!"

"That's the best yet," Pollyanna crowed.

"Oh, of course," John Pendleton said bitterly. "I can be glad too for all the rest, I suppose. The nurse and doctor and that confounded woman in the kitchen."

"Think how bad 'twould be if you didn't have them."

"It's bad enough lying here, and you expect me to be glad because the whole bunch expects me to pay them well."

" I CAN BE GLAD FOR ALL THE RES

POLLYANNA

Pollyanna frowned sympathetically. "That part is too bad, and when you've been saving your money all this time, buying fish balls and beans, denying yourself for the sake of the heathen. Nancy told me. She works for my Aunt Polly Harrington. I live with her. She's taken me to bring up on account of my mother, her sister, you know. After Father went to be with her in Heaven, I only had the ...es' Aid, so Aunt Polly took me," she said in a low

...dleton's face turned white. After a long ... "So you are Miss Polly Harrington's ... watched so closely Pollyanna felt

... her."

... mean it was Miss Polly

...?"

... sir. She said I-I ... she sent it."

... his head away and

" SO YOU ARE MISS POLLY HARRINGTON'S NIECE ?

Pollyanna tiptoed from the room.

"May I have the pleasure of seeing you home?" the doctor asked when she reached the steps.

"Thank you, sir. I just love to ride." She beamed. "Dr. Chilton, I should think being a doctor would be the very gladdest kind of a business there was."

"'Gladdest!' When I see so much suffering?" he cried.

She nodded. "I know, but you're *helping* it, and of course, you're glad you can."

The doctor's eyes filled with sudden, hot tears. His life was a singularly lonely one. He had no wife, no home but his two-room office in a boarding house. Looking into Pollyanna's shining eyes, he felt as if God's loving hand had been suddenly laid on his head in blessing. He knew, too, never again would a long day or night's weariness be quite without that new-found exaltation that had come through Pollyanna's eyes. "God bless you, little girl," he said unsteadily. He left her at her own door, smiled at Nancy who was sweeping the front porch, then drove away.

HE FELT AS IF GOD'S LOVING HAND HAD BEEN LAID ON HIS HEAD

"He's lovely, Nancy," Pollyanna said. "I told him I should think his business would be the very gladdest one."

"What! Goin' to see sick folks an' folks what ain't but thinks they is, which is worse?" Nancy frowned. "Oh, I know." Her face cleared. "He's just the opposite from what you told Mis' Snow, that she could be glad other folks wasn't like her—all sick. Well, the doctor can be glad he isn't like the sick ones he doctors!"

Pollyanna frowned. "Why, y-yes, but somehow I don't seem to like the sound of it—you do play the game so funny sometimes, Nancy." She sighed and went into the house.

"Who was that man who drove into the yard?" Aunt Polly sharply questioned.

"Dr. Chilton. Don't you know him?"

"Dr. Chilton! What was he doing—here?"

"He drove me home. I gave the jelly to Mr. Pendleton—"

"Pollyanna, he didn't think I sent it?"

"DR. CHILTON! WHAT WAS HE DOING—HERE?"

"Oh, no. I told him you didn't." Her aunt's face turned vivid pink. "Aunt Polly, you *said* to."

"I *said* for you to be sure he didn't think I sent it, which is quite different from *telling* him." She turned away.

"Dear me, I don't see the difference." Pollyanna went to hang her hat on the one particular hook upon which Aunt Polly said it must be hung.

On a rainy day about a week later, Miss Polly came in with her hair blown by the damp wind into kinks and curls, her cheeks pink. "Oh, Aunt Polly, you've got 'em, too!" She danced around. "Those darling black curls, like I'm going to have in Heaven. They're so pretty! Mayn't I do your hair like I did Mrs. Snow's and put in a flower? You'd be ever so much prettier that way." Miss Polly ignored her, although she wondered when anyone had ever cared to see her pretty. "Why did you go to the Ladies' Aid in that absurd fashion about the beggar boy?"

"He's not a beggar, and I didn't know it was absurd until I went and found out they'd rather hear about a little

"DEAR ME, I DON'T SEE THE DIFFERENCE"

India boy than see Jimmy grow. So then I wrote to my Ladies' Aiders, 'cause Jimmy is far away. I thought maybe he could be their little India boy the same as—Aunt Polly, was I your little India girl? And, you will let me do your hair, won't you?"

Aunt Polly put her hand to her throat, feeling the same helplessness she'd felt about the kitten and dog. "I—"

"You didn't say I couldn't, so I'm sure it means the other way 'round!" she said triumphantly. "Wait, and I'll get a comb." She dashed upstairs, Aunt Polly following. "Oh, this is nicer. Sit down, please. I'm so glad—" Miss Polly didn't finish her sentence. Ten eager but gentle fingers had her hair tumbling to her shoulders as soon as she sat down in the low chair before the dressing table. Pollyanna prattled on about how pretty her aunt's hair was and how much more she had than Mrs. Snow. "I'll make you so pretty everybody will just love to look at you," she promised.

"Pollyanna!" gasped a shocked voice. Patting and

POLLYANNA PRATTLED ON HOW PRETTY HER AUNT'S HAIR WAS

fixing cut off her protest. Pollyanna ran from the room, calling she had a secret and would be right back, and Miss Polly caught sight of herself in the mirror. Her face, not young, yet held beauty. Her eyes sparkled above her pink cheeks and the wonderfully becoming hairstyle amazed her. The next moment, Pollyanna returned, and slipped a blindfold over her eyes. "Pollyanna, what are you doing?" she demanded.

"I'll let you see in a moment." Pollyanna chuckled. She draped a fleecy lace shawl she'd found in the attic over her aunt's shoulders, then ran to pluck a belated red rose blooming on the trellis and tucked it into the soft dark waves. She snatched off the blindfold. "Now I reckon you'll be glad I dressed you up!"

For one dazed moment Miss Polly gazed, then looked around—and fled, with a low cry. Pollyanna saw in the direction of her aunt's last gaze the open window and the horse and gig turning into the driveway. Dr. Chilton called for her to come down. Pollyanna ran to find her

POLLY CAUGHT SIGHT OF HERSELF IN THE MIRROR

aunt, who moaned, "How could you rig me up like this—
to be seen!" She attacked her hair and pulled it so tightly
every curl vanished. Pollyanna's eyes filled, and she
stumbled out to the rig. And when she asked Aunt Polly
if Dr. Chilton could take her to see Mr. Pendleton, Miss
Polly Harrington told her to go, "like she didn't want me,"
Pollyanna told the doctor. "Didn't she look lovely, all
dressed up?"

"Yes—but never tell her I said so. She wouldn't be
glad. That's why she ran. Because she saw me," he said.

Today, John Pendleton greeted Pollyanna with a smile.
He brought out a box of treasures, curios he'd collected
in his years of travel and before she left, he asked her to
come often. "You remind me of someone I used to know."
he told her.

After supper that evening, Nancy said, "He took to you
'cause of *the mystery*. It's just like a book; I've read lots—
'Lady Maud's Secret' and 'The Lost Heir'. My stars and
stockings! He acted funny when he found out you were

"YES – BUT NEVER TELL HER I SAID SO"

Miss Polly's niece. I've got it, sure. *Mr. John Pendleton was Miss Polly Harrington's sweetheart!* Mr. Tom told me she had one, and he was livin' right here. They musta quarreled. An' if any pair wouldn't have no use for your 'glad' game and be cross as two sticks, it'd be them."

"But Nancy, if they loved each other, I should think they'd be glad to make up some time. Both of 'em all alone all these years."

"It would be a pretty slick piece of business if you could get 'em to play the game so they *would* be glad to make up. But, my land! Wouldn't folks stare! I guess there ain't much chance."

Pollyanna said nothing; but when she went into the house a little later, her face was very thoughtful.

"I GUESS THERE AIN'T MUCH CHANCE"

HE DID LIKE TO HEAR POLLYANNA TALK

6
Dancing Rainbows

As the warm August days passed, Pollyanna went often to the great house on Pendleton Hill but felt her visits weren't a success. John Pendleton talked and showed her strange and beautiful things, but he hated the rules and "regulatings" of his household. He did like to hear Pollyanna talk, but she was never sure she wouldn't look up and find him lying back on his pillow with the white, hurt look that always pained her. And she could never tell which—if any—of her words brought the look. She had tried twice now to tell him about the glad game but hadn't gotten past the beginning of what her father said before he changed the subject.

Pollyanna never doubted now that John Pendleton was once her Aunt Polly's sweetheart. With all the strength of her loving, loyal heart, she wished she could bring happiness into their—to her mind—miserably lonely lives. But how? When she mentioned Aunt Polly to John Pendleton, he just listened. Aunt Polly turned away when Pollyanna spoke of her visits to Pendleton Hill. She also acted bitter toward Dr. Chilton, and Pollyanna believed it was because he had seen her with the lace shawl, and the rose tucked into her hair. She wanted to call in Dr. Warren and refused to have Dr. Chilton when a severe cold shut Pollyanna up in the house one day.

"I'm glad I didn't need a doctor after all," Pollyanna told her aunt that evening. "Of course, I like Dr. Warren, but I like Dr. Chilton better, and he'd feel hurt. He wasn't really to blame for seeing you that day when I dressed you up so pretty."

"That will do. I really do not wish to discuss Dr. Chilton, or his feelings," reproved Miss Polly.

Toward the end of August, Pollyanna made an early morning call on John Pendleton. A flaming band of blue and gold and green edged with red and violet lay

"I LIKE DR. CHILTON BETTER"

across his pillow. "Why, Mr. Pendleton, it's a baby rainbow—a real rainbow come in to pay you a visit." She clapped her hands in delight. "How did it get in?"

He laughed grimly, out of sorts this morning. "Through the bevelled edge of that glass thermometer in the window. The sun shouldn't strike it at all, but it does in the morning."

"It's so pretty! My, if it were mine, I'd have it hang in the sun all day long. I shouldn't care that I couldn't tell how hot or cold it was. As if anybody would, when they're living all the time in a rainbow!"

John Pendleton laughed and rang a bell. When the elderly maid appeared, he ordered, "Nora, bring me one of the big brass candlesticks from the front drawing-room mantel."

"Yes, sir." She looked slightly dazed but soon returned, along with a musical tinkling sound as she advanced toward the bed. It came from the prism-shaped pendants encircling the old-fashioned

JOHN PENDLETON LAUGHED AND RANG A BELL

candelabrum in her hand.

"Now get string and fasten it to the sash-curtain fixtures of that window there. Take down the sash-curtain and let the string reach straight across the window from side to side. That will be all. Thank you," he said when she had carried out his directions. She left the room and he smiled at Pollyanna. "Bring me the candlestick, please."

She did and he slipped off the round dozen of pendants. "Now, my dear, hook them to the string. If you really want to live in a rainbow, I don't see but we'll have to have one!"

With each prism-shaped pendant Pollyanna hung, the room grew more beautiful, a fairyland that had once been a dreary bedroom. Dancing red and green, violet and orange, gold and blue on floor, walls, furniture, even the bed.

Pollyanna laughed joyously. "I reckon the sun himself is trying to play the game now. Oh, I wish I had

THE ROOM GREW MORE BEAUTIFUL

a lot of those things, for Aunt Polly and Mrs. Snow and lots of folks!"

"What do you mean, the game?"

"Oh, I forgot you don't know." She settled down and told John Pendleton the whole story, starting with the crutches that should have been a doll. She kept her gaze on the dancing rainbows from the swaying pendants in the sunlit windows and didn't see his face.

When she finished he said in a low, unsteady voice, "I'm thinking the very finest prism of them all is yourself."

"Oh, but I don't show beautiful red and green and purple when the sun shines through me, Mr. Pendleton!"

"Don't you?"

Pollyanna wondered why tears came to his eyes. "No," she said mournfully. "The sun doesn't make anything but freckles out of me!"

Pollyanna entered school in September. Examinations

POLLYANNA ENTERED SCHOOL IN SEPTEMBER

showed her to be well advanced for her age, and she was soon a happy member of a class of boys and girls of her own age. She confessed that going to school *was* living, even though she'd had her doubts. Until now, her father had taught her at home.

She didn't forget her old friends, but couldn't give them as much time. Of them all, John Pendleton was most dissatisfied. One Saturday afternoon, he said impatiently, "I don't see anything of you nowadays. How would you like to come and live with me?"

Pollyanna laughed. Mr. Pendleton was such a funny man. "I thought you didn't like to have folks 'round."

He made a wry face. "That was before you taught me to play that wonderful game of yours."

Pollyanna kept her gaze fixed on the dog. "You don't play the game right, *ever*. You know you don't."

"That's why I want you, little girl—to help me play it. Will you come?"

Pollyanna turned in surprise. "I can't. You know

"YOU KNOW I CAN'T. WHY, I AM AUNT POLLY'S"

I can't. Why, I am Aunt Polly's!"

"You're no more hers than—" he said fiercely. "Would you come if she would let you?"

"But she's been so good to me. She took me in when I didn't have anybody left but the Ladies' Aid—"

A spasm crossed his face, and he said in a low voice, "Pollyanna, long years ago I loved somebody very much and hoped to bring her to this house. Well, I didn't. Never mind why. Ever since this great gray pile of stone has been a house. It takes a woman's hand or a child's presence to make a home, and I have not had either. Now will you come, my dear?"

Pollyanna sprang up, face radiant. "You mean you wish you'd had that woman's hand and heart all this time? Why, I'm so glad. Now you can take both of us and everything will be lovely."

"Take—you—both?" he repeated, dazedly.

A faint doubt crossed Pollyanna's countenance. "Aunt Polly isn't won over, but I'm sure she will be if

"AUNT POLLY ISN'T WON OVER..."

you tell her as you did me, then we'd both come, of course."

"Pollyanna, what *are* you talking about?" he said gently.

"Why, you said you had wanted Aunt Polly's hand and heart all these years to make a home, and—"

A cry burst from his throat. "Pollyanna, for Heaven's sake, say nothing of what I asked you—yet," he begged.

Pollyanna dimpled into a sunny smile. "Of course not! Just as if I didn't know you'd rather tell her yourself!" She ran out, and Dr. Chilton came in a moment later.

"What's up?" he demanded when he laid fingers on his patient's galloping pulse.

"Overdose of your tonic, I guess." John Pendleton watched Pollyanna fly down the driveway.

On the way home from Sunday School the next day, Dr. Chilton overtook Pollyanna in his rig. "John

DR. CHILTON OVERTOOK POLLYANNA IN HIS RIG

Pendleton sent a special request for you to go see him this afternoon."

"I know. I'll go."

"I don't know if I should let you, after yesterday. You seemed more upsetting than soothing." His eyes twinkled.

"'Twasn't me, but Aunt Polly."

"Your—aunt!" he blurted.

"Yes, just like a story. I'm going to tell you. I'm sure he meant just not to tell Aunt Polly and wouldn't mind your knowing. He wants to tell her himself; sweethearts do."

"Sweethearts!" Dr. Chilton gave the reins a sharp jerk.

"I didn't know until Nancy told me, but Aunt Polly had a sweetheart years ago, and they quarreled. We didn't know who, at first, but we figured out it must be Mr. Pendleton."

The doctor suddenly relaxed. "I didn't know."

"SWEETHEARTS!"

"Yes, and it's all coming out so lovely. If Mr. Pendleton wants to make up the quarrel, surely Aunt Polly will, and we'll both go there to live—he asked me, you know."

She found a very nervous John Pendleton waiting for her that afternoon. "Pollyanna, I've been trying all night to puzzle out what you meant by all that, yesterday—about my wanting your Aunt Polly's hand and heart here all those years."

"Why, because you were sweethearts. I was so glad you still felt that way now."

"Sweethearts? Your Aunt Polly and I?"

Pollyanna opened her eyes wide at the obvious surprise in his voice. "Why, Mr. Pendleton, Nancy said you were!"

"Never!"

Pollyanna almost sobbed. "And it was all so splendid. I'd have been so glad to come with Aunt Polly. Now I can't. I'm hers."

POLLYANNA ALMOST SOBBED

The man turned fiercely. "Before you were hers, you were your mother's. I hadn't meant to tell you, but it was your mother's hand and heart that I wanted long years ago." His face grew white. "I loved your mother, but she didn't love me. After a time, she went away with your father. My whole world turned black. For long years, I have been a cross, crabbed, unlovable, unloved old man—though I'm not yet sixty. Then one day, you danced into my life like one of the prisms you love so well, with dashes of purple and gold and scarlet of your own cheeriness. You brightened my life. When I found out who you were, I never wanted to see you and be reminded of your mother. Then I changed. Pollyanna, now won't you come?"

"But Mr. Pendleton, there's Aunt Polly." Her eyes blurred with tears.

"What about me?" He waved impatiently. "How can I be glad about anything without you? And I'd make you happy. All my money would go to grant your wishes."

"WHAT ABOUT ME?"

Pollyanna looked shocked. "As if I'd let you spend the money you've saved for the heathen. Besides, anyone with a lot of money doesn't need me. You're making other folks so glad giving them things, you can't help being glad, like those prisms you gave Mrs. Snow and me, and the gold piece you gave Nancy for her birthday—"

His face was very red now. "'Twasn't much, and it was because of you. Of course, Aunt Polly's been good to you, but she doesn't want you half so much as I do. I'll wager Miss Polly doesn't know how to be glad for anything. She does her duty but she isn't the glad kind. Just ask her to let you come, and you'll see. Little girl, I want you so!"

"All right, I'll ask her," she said wistfully. "I'm glad I didn't mention except to the doctor about her coming."

"Dr. Chilton?" Pollyanna wondered why he gave a sudden strange little laugh.

"ALL RIGHT, I'LL ASK HER"

"I SAID YOUR AUNT WAS WORRIED"

7
Rejoice and be Glad

The sky had fast darkened with an approaching thunder shower when Pollyanna hurried down the hill from John Pendleton's house. Half-way home, she met Nancy with an umbrella, although by that time the clouds had shifted their position and the shower was not so imminent.

"Guess it's goin' 'round to the north." Nancy eyed the sky critically. "I thought 'twas, all the time, but Miss Polly wanted me to come with this. She was worried about ye."

"Was she?" murmured Pollyanna abstractedly, looking at the clouds.

Nancy sniffed a little. "You don't seem to notice what I said," she complained. "I said your aunt was *worried.*"

"Oh," sighed Pollyanna, suddenly remembering the

question she had promised to ask her aunt. "I'm sorry. I didn't mean to scare her."

"Well, I'm glad," Nancy retorted. "I am, I am."

Pollyanna stared. "*Glad* that Aunt Polly was scared about me? Why, Nancy, that isn't the way to play the game," she objected.

"There wasn't no game in it." Nancy sniffed again. "You don't seem to sense what it means to have Miss Polly worried about ye, child!" She tossed her head. "It means she's at last gettin' down somewheres near human—like folks; an' that she ain't just doin' her duty by ye all the time."

"Why, Nancy, Aunt Polly always does her duty," the scandalized Pollyanna said.

"She does but she's somethin' more, now, since you came."

Pollyanna's brows drew into a troubled frown. "There, that's what I was going to ask you. Do you think Aunt Polly likes to have me here? Would she

"DO YOU THINK AUNT POLLY LIKES TO HAVE ME HERE?"

mind—if—I wasn't here any more?"

Nancy threw a quick look into the little girl's absorbed face. She had expected to be asked this question and dreaded it. How could she answer honestly without cruelly hurting Pollyanna? Now she whispered a prayer of thanks for Miss Polly's umbrella-sending and welcomed the question with open arms. With a clean conscience, she could set the love-hungry little girl's heart at rest.

"Likes to have ye? Would she miss ye?" she indignantly cried. "That's just what I was tellin'! Didn't she send me posthaste with an umbrella 'cause she saw a little cloud in the sky? Didn't she make me tote all your things downstairs so you could have the pretty room you wanted?" With a choking cough, she went on. "It ain't just things I can put my fingers on," she said breathlessly. "It's little ways you've been softenin' her—the dog, the cat, the way she speaks to me; oh, there's lots of things. Why, Miss Pollyanna,

"IT'S LITTLE WAYS YOU'VE BEEN SOFTENIN' HER"

there ain't no tellin' how she'd miss ye if ye wasn't here."

Sudden joy illuminated Pollyanna's face. "Oh, Nancy, I'm so glad—*glad*—GLAD! You don't know how glad I am Aunt Polly wants me." She thought of it again when she climbed the stairs to her bedroom a little later. "I always knew I wanted to live with her. As if I'd leave her now! I reckon maybe I didn't know quite how much I wanted Aunt Polly—to want to live with *me*."

She sighed. She hated having to tell Mr. Pendleton she couldn't live with him. She was sorry, too, for all his long, lonely years spent grieving because of her mother. She pictured the great, gray house as it would be when its owner was well and alone again. If only she could find someone who— With a cry of joy, she lost the ache in her heart and hurried up the hill to John Pendleton's house. She found him in the great dim library, his long, thin hands lying idle and his faithful

"I ALWAYS KNEW I WANTED TO LIVE WITH HER"

little dog at his feet. "Well, Pollyanna, is it to be the 'glad game' with me all the rest of my life?" he asked gently.

"Oh, yes," Pollyanna cried. "I've thought of the very gladdest kind of thing for you to do, and—"

"With *you*?" His mouth grew stern.

"N-no, but—"

"Pollyanna, you aren't going to say no," a deep voice interrupted.

"I've got to. Aunt Polly—"

"Did she refuse to let you come?"

"I-I didn't ask her," stammered the miserable little girl.

"Pollyanna!"

"I couldn't, sir, truly. I found out she wants me, and I want to stay, too," she added bravely.

Only the snapping of the wood fire in the grate broke the silence. At last he said, almost inaudibly, "I won't ask you again."

"I WON'T ASK YOU AGAIN"

Pollyanna took heart. "Oh, but you don't know the rest of it," she reminded him eagerly. "You said only a woman's hand and heart or a child's presence could make a home. I can get it for you—a child's presence, I mean, but not me."

"As if I'd have anyone but you!" he said indignantly.

"You will when you know. You're so good and kind. Why, think of the prisms and gold pieces and all that money you save for the heathen, and—"

"Pollyanna!" he interrupted savagely. "I've tried to tell you. There is no money for the heathen. I've never sent a penny to them in my life. So there!" He raised his chin and braced himself for her grief and disappointment. To his amazement, only surprised joy sprang to her eyes.

"Oh, I'm so glad!" She clapped her hands. "Not that I'm not sorry for the heathen but I can't help being glad you don't want the little India boys, because all the rest wanted them. I'm so glad you'd rather have Jimmy

"I CAN GET IT FOR YOU – A CHILD'S PRESENCE"

Bean. Now I know you'll take him."

"Take—*who*?" John Pendleton sat up as if he'd been poked.

"Jimmy Bean. He's the child's presence, you know, and he'll be so glad. I had to tell him last week even my Ladies' Aid out West wouldn't take him, and he was so disappointed. When he hears of this, he'll be so glad!"

"Will he?" John Pendleton scowled. "Well, I won't. I prefer being lonesome to having any child around but you."

Pollyanna was almost crying, but she suddenly remembered what Nancy had said weeks before. "Maybe you think a nice, live little boy wouldn't be better than that old, dead skeleton Nancy said you keep somewhere, but I think it would!"

"*Skeleton?* Why, what—" Suddenly, he threw back his head and laughed so heartily Pollyanna began to cry from pure nervousness. When he saw that, his face grew grave at once. "I suspect you're right," he said

"TAKE—WHO?"

gently. "But sometimes we're apt to cling to our skeletons. However, suppose you tell me more about this boy." Perhaps her story softened the heart already stirred by Pollyanna and her faith. In any event, she left carrying an invitation to bring Jimmy Bean to call at the Pendleton mansion the next Saturday. "I'm sure you'll like him," she said in parting. "I do want him to have a home and folks that care, you know."

That same afternoon, the Reverend Paul Ford, sick at heart from the quarreling, backbiting, scandal, and jealousy among his congregation, went to Pendleton woods seeking God's peace. Reverend Ford had pleaded, rebuked, and ignored the trouble, always fervently praying. He had failed. Conditions had continued to worsen until many left off attending and dropped out of the choir and Ladies' Aid because of gossip and hurt feelings. The Sunday School superintendent and two teachers had just resigned. Either something must be done, or God's work would be left

REVEREND PAUL FORD WENT TO PENDLETON WOODS

undone, and the message of salvation overcome by pettiness.

He took sermon notes from his pocket and read aloud, "'But woe unto you, scribes and Pharisees, hypocrites....'" After the end of the passage given in his bitter voice, even the birds and squirrels hushed. Did he dare use those words and follow with the denunciation so many deserved? He moaned and flung himself down at the foot of a tree, his face in his hands.

Pollyanna found him there on her way home. "Oh, Reverend Ford, you haven't broken *your* leg, have you?"

He sat up and dropped his hands, trying to smile. "I haven't broken anything doctors can mend."

Her face changed. Sympathy glowed in her eyes. "I know what you mean. Something plagues you. Father used to feel like that, lots of times. I reckon most ministers do, such a lot depends on 'em." She paused. "Do you like being a minister?"

"I HAVEN'T BROKEN ANYTHING DOCTORS CAN MEND"

POLLYANNA

"Why, what an odd question." He looked startled.

"It's just the way you look, like Father used to look sometimes, sad-like. When I asked him if he was glad, he said he wouldn't stay a minister a minute if 'twasn't for the rejoicing texts." She laughed. "That's what he called 'em, but the Bible didn't name 'em that. It's all those that begin with 'Be glad in the Lord,' or 'Rejoice greatly,' or 'Shout for joy.' Such a lot of 'em. Once when Father felt specially bad, he counted 'em. There were eight hundred."

"Eight hundred!" An odd look came to the minister's face.

"Yes. He said he felt better right away that first day he thought to count 'em. He said if God took the trouble to tell us eight hundred times to be glad and rejoice, He must want us to do it. Father felt ashamed he hadn't done it more, and the rejoicing texts got to be a comfort when things went wrong. Why, those texts made Father think of the game he began with me when

"THERE WERE EIGHT HUNDRED"

the crutches came." She happily told the bewildered Reverend Ford the whole story. Later, they descended the hill, hand-in-hand.

That evening, the minister sat in his study thinking. A picture rose in his mind: a discouraged, poor, sick, worried missionary minister almost alone in the world who pored over his Bible to find how many times his Lord and Master had told him to rejoice. His gaze lighted on a magazine with the illustration of a wise father who said to his son who had refused to fill the woodbox that morning, "Tom, I'm sure you'll be glad to go and bring in some wood for your mother." Without a word, Tom went—because his father plainly showed he expected him to do right. The story went on, saying that if the father had said, "Tom, I overheard what you said to your mother this morning, and I'm ashamed of you. Go at once and fill the woodbox," in all probability the woodbox would be empty yet.

"What men and women need is encouragement,"

'WHAT MEN AND WOMEN NEED IS ENCOURAGEMENT'

the story concluded. "Tell your son Tom you *know* he'll be glad to fill that woodbox—then watch him start, alert and interested."

"God helping me, I'll do it," cried the minister softly. "I'll tell all my Toms I *know* they'll be glad to fill that woodbox. I'll keep them so busy and filled with joy in serving the Lord they won't have time to look at their neighbors' woodboxes!"

The next Sunday, the Reverend Paul Ford's text was one of Pollyanna's shining eight hundred: "Be glad in the LORD, and rejoice, ye righteous: and shout for joy, all ye that are upright in heart" (Psalm 32:11, KJV).

REVEREND FORD'S TEXT WAS ONE OF POLLYANNA'S EIGHT HUNDRED

"I SHOULD THINK YOU COULD GET 'EM"

8
A Terrible Accident

One day Mrs. Snow asked Pollyanna to go to Dr. Chilton's office to get the name of a medicine she'd forgotten.

"I've never been to your home before," she told him.

"It's a pretty poor apology for a home. They're just rooms." The doctor smiled sadly.

"I know. It takes a woman's hand and heart or a child's presence to make a home," she said sympathetically. "Mr. Pendleton told me. Why don't you get a woman's hand and heart? Or if Mr. Pendleton doesn't want Jimmy Bean, maybe you'd take him. Oh, I forgot." She turned red. "It wasn't Aunt Polly Mr. Pendleton loved long ago. I made a mistake. So we aren't going there to live. But why don't you get a woman's hand and heart, Dr. Chilton?"

"They're not always to be had for the asking."

Pollyanna frowned. "I should think you could get 'em," she argued. Her eyes opened wide. "Why, you didn't try to get somebody's hand and heart once, like Mr. Pendleton— and couldn't, did you?"

Dr. Chilton abruptly got to his feet. "Never mind about that, child. Don't let other people's troubles worry your head. Suppose you run back now to Mrs. Snow with the name of the medicine, and the directions how she is to take it."

Pollyanna turned toward the door. From the hallway, she called back, face suddenly alight, "I'm glad 'twasn't my mother's hand and heart you wanted and couldn't get, Dr. Chilton. Goodbye!"

The accident occurred on the last day of October. Pollyanna, hurrying home from school, crossed the road at what she thought was a safe distance in front of a swiftly approaching motor car.

Just what happened, no one could tell afterward. Neither was there anyone found who could tell why it happened or who was to blame. Pollyanna, however, was

THE ACCIDENT OCCURRED ON THE LAST DAY OF OCTOBER

borne limp and unconscious at five o'clock into the little room so dear to her. A white-faced Aunt Polly and a weeping Nancy undressed her tenderly and put her to bed while Dr. Warren, summoned by telephone, hurried from the village as fast as another motor car could bring him.

"Ye didn't need to more'n look at her aunt's face," Nancy sobbed to Old Tom in the garden, "to see 'twasn't duty that was eatin' her. Hands don't shake an' eyes don't look is if ye was tryin' to hold back the Angel of Death himself, when you're just doin' your *duty*."

"Is she hurt bad?" The old man's voice shook.

"There ain't no tellin'," Nancy cried some more. "She's all white an' so still she might easy be dead but Miss Polly said she 'twasn't; she kept a-listenin' an' a feelin' for her heartbeats an' her breath. Drat it! To think of the evil-smellin' thing runnin' down our little girl! I always hated them, anyhow, I did, I did!"

"But where's she hurt?"

"I don't know," moaned Nancy. "There's a little cut

"IS SHE HURT BAD?"

on her blessed head, but 'tain't bad—Miss Polly says. She's afraid it's infernally Pollyanna's hurt."

"I guess you mean in*ter*nally," Old Tom said dryly. "She's hurt infernally, all right, plague take that autymobile."

Nancy turned away. "Seems as if I can't stand it till that doctor gets out o' there. I wish I had the biggest washin' I ever see, I do, I do!" She wrung her hands helplessly.

The doctor looked grave when he did come out. No bones appeared to be broken, but he shook his head and said time alone could tell. Pollyanna remained unconscious and not until before noon the next day did she awaken.

"Why, Aunt Polly, it's daytime! Why don't I get up?" she cried and tried to lift herself from the pillow. "Why can't I get up? What's the matter?"

"Don't try just yet," Aunt Polly soothed but the white-capped young woman standing by the window

"DON'T TRY, JUST YET," AUNT POLLY SOOTHED

out of Pollyanna's sight nodded and silently mouthed, "Tell her."

Miss Polly could scarcely speak for the lump in her throat. "You were hurt last night by the automobile. Never mind that. Auntie wants you to rest and go to sleep again."

"Hurt? Oh yes, I ran." Pollyanna lifted her hand to her forehead, acting dazed. "Why, it's done up—and it hurts!"

"Just rest."

"But Aunt Polly, I feel so funny and so bad! My legs feel so—so queer—only they don't *feel* at all!"

With an imploring look at the nurse, Miss Polly struggled to her feet and turned away. The nurse quickly came forward. "Suppose you let me talk to you now," she said cheerily. "I'm Miss Hunt and I've come to help your aunt take care of you. The very first thing is for you to swallow these little white pills for me."

Pollyanna's eyes grew a bit wild. "But I don't want to

"MY LEGS FEEL SO-SO QUEER!"

be taken care of. I want to get up. Can't I go to school tomorrow?"

Aunt Polly stifled a cry, but Miss Hunt smiled. "Maybe not quite that soon. Now, swallow these pills and see what they'll do."

"All right, but I *must* go the day after tomorrow. There are examinations." She swallowed the medicine, spoke of the automobile and how her head ached but soon her voice trailed off under the blessed influence of the little white pills.

Pollyanna did not go to school "tomorrow" or "the day after." She didn't realize this except in the few moments of full consciousness between periods of pain and fever. She had to be told all over about the accident. "So it's hurt I am and not sick," she sighed. "I'm glad. I'd rather have broken legs like Mr. Pendleton's than lifelong invalids like Mrs. Snow. Broken legs get well and life-long invalids don't."

She blinked at the dancing band of colors on her ceiling

"SO IT'S HURT I AM AND NOT SICK"

that came from one of the prisms in the window. She prattled about how glad she was she didn't have smallpox or measles or appendicitis or whooping cough, then said, "I'm 'most glad I was hurt!" When Miss Polly looked shocked, she quickly added, "Since I've been hurt you've called me 'dear' lots of times. Oh, Aunt Polly, I'm so glad you belong to me!"

That afternoon, Nancy raced to find Old Tom who was cleaning harnesses in the barn. "Oh, Mr. Tom, you'll never guess what's happened! John Pendleton is callin' on Miss Polly, after all these years. I had it figured he was the one you told me about—Miss Polly's sweetheart, but I know now it was Miss Pollyanna's mother. Miss Polly's been hatin' John Pendleton for years 'cause folks said she was runnin' after him, just 'cause she felt sorry about Miss Jennie not lovin' him an' tried to be nice to him. Anyway, he's here."

In the parlor, Mr. Pendleton turned toward Polly Harrington, whose face remained cold and reserved. "I

"OH, AUNT POLLY, I'M SO GLAD YOU BELONG TO ME!"

called to ask for Pollyanna. How is she?"

"Dr. Warren has arranged with a New York specialist who is coming for a consultation." She drew a long breath. "She has an injury to the spine which has seemed to cause—paralysis from the hips down."

A low cry came, then John Pendleton brokenly asked, "How does Pollyanna take it?"

"She doesn't know, and I *can't* tell her. She thinks her legs are broken and is glad they aren't like Mrs. Snow. When she talks like that it seems as if I should die." Her face twisted, and Mr. Pendleton felt sympathy for her.

"Miss Harrington, I wonder if you know how hard I tried to get Pollyanna to come live with me. I wanted to adopt her legally and make her my heir. I am fond of her for both her sake and her mother's." Miss Polly sat stone still. "She wouldn't come. She said you'd been good to her, and she thought you wanted her to stay as she wanted to stay with you." He turned toward the door.

She came and thrust a shaking hand to him. "When

"SHE HAS - PARALYSIS FROM THE HIPS DOWN"

the specialist comes, and I know anything definite, I'll let you hear from me. Thank you for coming. Pollyanna will be—pleased."

The next day she told her niece, "We want another doctor to examine you and help you get well faster."

A joyous light came to Pollyanna's face. "Oh, Aunt Polly, I'd so love to have Dr. Chilton!" The light died when her aunt turned white, then red, then white and told her it wasn't Dr. Chilton, but a famous New York doctor who knew a great deal about hurts like hers. All Pollyanna's pleading would not change Aunt Polly's mind, and the disconsolate little girl sadly listened while her aunt repeated she'd do anything for her—except call Dr. Chilton. She proved it by bringing Fluffy and Buffy up to tumble on the bed, wearing her hair in curls and donning ribbons and lace.

Nancy kept Old Tom posted and found he knew the glad game. "I was growlin' one day 'cause I was so bent up and crooked, and she ups and says I can be glad I don't

"I'D SO LOVE TO HAVE DR.CHILTON!"

have to stoop so far to do the weedin'!" They marveled that everyone—except Miss Polly—knew and played the game.

Pollyanna continued to tell Nancy how glad she'd be to go back to school, or to see Mrs. Snow, call on Mr. Pendleton and ride with Dr. Chilton. She didn't seem to realize all this "gladness" was in the future, not the present, but Nancy did realize and cried about it when she was alone.

The specialist, Dr. Mead, came, tall, broad-shouldered and kind. Pollyanna liked him and told him he looked like *her* doctor, Dr. Chilton; that Dr. Warren was Aunt Polly's doctor. "She said you knew more about legs like mine," she said confidingly. "I can be glad for that. Do you?"

"Only time can tell that, little girl." He turned a grave face toward Dr. Warren who had just come to the bedside.

Everyone said afterward the cat did it. Certainly, if Fluffy hadn't poked an insistent paw and nose against

EVERYONE SAID AFTERWARD THE CAT DID IT

Pollyanna's unlocked door, it wouldn't have swung noiselessly open. And if it hadn't been open, Pollyanna wouldn't have overheard her aunt's words.

In the hall, the two doctors, nurse, and Miss Polly stood talking. Through the open door came Aunt Polly's agonized exclamation. "Doctor, not that. You don't mean—the child—will *never walk* again!"

"Aunt Polly, Aunt Polly!" Pollyanna's terrified voice sent her aunt into the first faint of her life. The nurse choked out, "She heard!" and ran into the bedroom where a purring gray cat vainly tried to attract the white-faced, wild-eyed little girl's attention. "I want Aunt Polly," she repeated again and again. "I want her to tell me 'tisn't true." She looked at the nurse and cried, "It *is* true!"

"The doctor could be mistaken," the nurse quavered.

"But Aunt Polly said he knew! How can I go to school or to see Mrs. Snow or Mr. Pendleton?" She sobbed. "If I can't walk, how can I ever be glad for *anything*? Father said things might always be worse, but I don't see how anything can."

"SHE HEARD!"

"SHE CAN'T PLAY IT HERSELF"

9
Everyone Plays but Pollyanna

"You mean Pollyanna knows?" John Pendleton paused.

"Yes, 'twas that dratted cat," Nancy bowed her head miserably. Sent to tell him the news, she hadn't even looked about the House of Mystery while waiting for him to appear. "What worries her is that she can't seem to be glad—maybe you don't know about her game, sir."

"The 'glad game'? Oh yes, she told me."

"She's told it to most folks an' now she can't play it herself. She says she can't think of a thing to be glad about this not walkin.'" Nancy shifted and he growled, "Why should she?"

"That's the way I felt, too, till I happened to think it'd be easier if she could, so I tried to remind her how she told Mis' Snow and the rest. But the poor little lamb just cries and says it's easy to tell life-long invalids to be glad, but it ain't the same when it's her." She broke off. "I must be goin', sir. I couldn't be tellin' Miss Pollyanna that you'd seen Jimmy Bean again, I s'pose, sir? That's one of the things she's feelin' bad about. She said she'd taken him to see you once but didn't think he showed off very well, and she was afraid you'd think he wouldn't make a very nice child's presence, after all. Maybe you know what she means, I didn't."

"I know what she means, but I haven't seen him."

"All right, sir. It's just that now she can't show he really was a lovely child's presence, drat that autymobile!" Nancy fled.

Before long, the entire town of Beldingsville knew the great New York doctor had said Pollyanna Whittier would never walk again. Never before had the town been so stirred. Everyone knew the piquant, little freckle-faced girl who always had a smile, and almost everybody knew of the glad game. In kitchens, and over backyard fences, on street corners, and in stores, women wept and men gravely talked. But when word came, Pollyanna be-

NEVER BEFORE HAD THE TOWN BEEN SO STIRRED

moaned most of all that she couldn't seem to play her beloved game, the same thought came to her friends. Miss Polly Harrington began to receive calls from those who had never called before, many of whom she hadn't supposed her niece knew at all.

Some came in and sat down for a stiff five or ten minutes. Some stood awkwardly on the porch. Some brought a book, or a bunch of flowers, or a dainty to tempt the palate. Some frankly cried or turned their backs and furiously blew their noses. But all inquired anxiously for the injured little girl and sent messages that bewildered Aunt Polly and stirred her to action.

John Pendleton said to tell her he'd seen Jimmy Bean and that hereafter he'd be Mr. Pendleton's boy; that he knew she'd be *glad* he planned to adopt Jimmy.

Adopt Jimmy Bean? Miss Polly stood in the middle of the floor half dazed, but Pollyanna's wistful face flamed into sudden joy when she heard the wonderful news.

"Glad? I reckon I am. Now he'll have the child's

ADOPT JIMMY BEAN?

presence." She blushed painfully. "He told me once only a woman's hand and heart or a child's presence could make a–a home."

"Oh—I see," Miss Polly said gently. She suddenly realized some of the pressure Pollyanna had felt when John Pendleton asked her to be the "child's presence" and transform his great pile of gray stone into a home. Her eyes stung.

"Dr. Chilton says so, too," she remarked.

Miss Polly turned with a start. *"Dr. Chilton!* How do you know that?"

"'Twas when he said he lived in just rooms, you know—not a home. I asked him why he didn't get 'em when he looked so sorrowful. First, he didn't say anything then he said very low you couldn't always get 'em for the asking."

Miss Polly turned back toward the window, cheeks unnaturally pink.

"On another day he said low, but I heard, that he'd give

"...YOU COULDN'T ALWAYS GET 'EM FOR THE ASKING"

all the world if he did have one woman's hand and heart. Why, Aunt Polly, what's the matter?"

"Nothing, dear. I was just changing the position of this prism," said Aunt Polly, whose whole face now flamed.

One afternoon, Milly Snow called. She blushed and looked embarrassed when Miss Polly entered the room but stammered, "I came to inquire for the little girl."

"You are very kind. She is about the same. How is your mother?" Miss Polly wearily said.

"That's what I came to tell you, to ask you to tell Miss Pollyanna. We think it's so awful she can't play the game after all she's done for us, and we thought if she knew what she *had* done for us that it would help because she could be a little glad—" She helplessly stopped.

"I don't think I quite understand, Milly. What is it you want me to tell my niece?"

"Make her see what she's done for us. She knows, a little. But Mother is so different; you know, nothing was ever right before. Now she lets me keep the shades up and

"MAKE HER SEE WHAT SHE'S DONE FOR U

she takes interest in how she looks and is knitting baby blankets for fairs and hospitals and has prisms make dancing rainbows in her room, and it's all because of Miss Pollyanna." She hastily rose. "You'll tell her?"

"Of course." But Miss Polly wondered how much of this amazing tale she could remember.

With every visitor, the curious messages crept into Polly Harrington's presence, to her complete puzzlement.

One day the little Widow Benton, who always wore black and was the saddest woman in town, called. Today she wore a knot of pale blue at her throat. She spoke of her grief and horror at the accident and diffidently asked if she might see Pollyanna.

"I'm sorry, but she sees no one yet. A little later, perhaps."

Mrs. Benton wiped her eyes, rose, and turned to go. But after she'd almost reached the hall door she came ~ck hurriedly. "Miss Harrington, perhaps you'd give her

"I'M SORRY, BUT SHE SEES NO ONE YET"

a message. Please tell her I've put on *this*." She touched the blue bow at her throat. "The little girl has been trying for so long to make me wear some color. She said Freddy would be so glad to see it. He's all I have now. The others—" She shook her head and turned away. "If you'll just tell Pollyanna, *she'll* understand."

Later that same day another widow came, at least she wore black garments.

"I'm Mrs. Tarbell, a stranger to you," she began. "But I'm not a stranger to your niece. I've been at the hotel all summer and every day I've had to take long walks for my health. I was very sad when I came up here; then I met her on one of my walks. When I heard of the accident and how unhappy she was 'cause she couldn't be glad any longer, why, I just had to come. I-I want you to give her a message for me. Just tell her Mrs. Tarbell is glad now. I know it sounds odd, but if you'll pardon me, I'd rather not explain. Pollyanna will know just what I mean." She took her leave.

"JUST TELL HER MRS. TARBELL IS GLAD NOW"

Thoroughly mystified, Miss Polly hurried upstairs to her niece's room. "Pollyanna, do you know a Mrs. Tarbell?"

"Oh, yes. I love her. She's sick and awfully sad. We used to take walks together." Two big tears rolled down her cheeks.

"Well, she's just been here, dear. She said to tell you Mrs. Tarbell is glad now."

Pollyanna softly clapped her hands. "Did she really say that? Oh, I'm so glad!"

"But Pollyanna, what did she mean?"

"Why, it's the game, and—" She stopped short, fingers to her lips.

"What game?"

"N-nothing much, Aunt Polly; that is, I can't tell it unless I tell other things I-I'm not allowed to speak of." The obvious distress in her face kept her aunt from further questions, but the climax came when a flashy young woman in cheap jewelry and high heels, hair too yellow

SHE STOPPED SHORT

and cheeks too pink, came to call. Aunt Polly knew her by reputation and that such a woman dared come to her home angered Miss Harrington.

"May I see Pollyanna?" the visitor defiantly asked.

"No." Something in the tear-stained face made her add that her niece was allowed no visitors.

The woman hesitated. "I'm Mrs. Tom Payson and I presume you've heard of me—most of the good people in the town have—and maybe some of the things you've heard ain't true. Never mind that. When I heard of the accident, I wished I could give the little girl my two well legs." She cleared her throat.

"Maybe you don't know, but I've seen a good deal of that little girl of yours. We live on the Pendleton Hill road, and she goes by but sometimes comes in and plays with the kids. She didn't suspect her kind of folks don't generally call on my kind. Maybe if they did call more, Miss Harrington, there wouldn't be so many of my kind," she bitterly said. "Anyway, she came, and it didn't hurt

"I PRESUME YOU'VE HEARD OF ME"

her, but she did us a lot of good.

"My man and me were reckoning on getting a divorce but when we heard about Pollyanna's never walking again, and thought how she used to come and sit on our doorstep and laugh and be glad—she even tried to teach us the game and how to be glad—anyway, we're going to try to play and maybe it will help her feel glad. I don't know yet how it will help us but will you tell her?"

"Yes," Miss Polly said a bit faintly. She held out her hand. "Mrs. Payson, thank you for coming."

The defiance left the caller's face. She blindly clutched the outstretched hand, turned, and fled.

The door scarcely closed behind her before Miss Polly confronted her hired girl in the kitchen. "Nancy! *Will* you tell me about this absurd 'game' the town is playing and everyone's babbling about? Why does everyone from Milly Snow to Mrs. Tom Payson send word they're playing it? As near as I can judge, half the town are putting on blue ribbons or stopping family quarrels all because of

"WILL YOU TELL ME ABOUT THIS ABSURD 'GAME'?"

Pollyanna. I tried to ask her but can't make much headway. Now *will* you tell me what it all means?"

To her surprise, Nancy burst into tears. "It means that ever since last June that blessed child has just been makin' the whole town glad an' now they're turnin' 'round an' tryin' to make her a little glad, too."

"Glad of what?"

"Just glad! That's the game."

Miss Polly stamped her foot. "*What* game?"

Between sobs Nancy told the whole poignant story; of the crutches that came when Pollyanna wanted a doll; how Reverend Whittier made a "glad game" when the child cried, telling her she could be glad they didn't need them. "You'd be surprised to find out how cute it works, ma'am," Nancy eagerly continued. "She's made me glad I'm Nancy and not Hephzibah and for Monday mornin's that I used to hate 'cause of all the work—she said I could be glad 'cause another wouldn't come for a whole week!" She added, "She hasn't told

NANCY TOLD THE WHOLE POIGNANT STORY

you 'cause 'twas her father's game."

"Well, I know someone who'll play it now," Miss Polly choked, which made Nancy stare in disbelief.

"WELL, I KNOW SOMEONE WHO'LL PLAY IT NOW"

"SHE SAID IT WOULD MAKE YOU GLAD TO KNOW"

10
Gladsome News

A little later in Pollyanna's room after the nurse left, Miss Polly asked if Pollyanna remembered Mrs. Payson.

"I reckon I do! She lives on the way to Mr. Pendleton's, and she's got the prettiest little girl baby three years old and a boy 'most five. She's awfully nice and so's her husband, but they don't seem to know how nice each other is. They're poor, too, and don't even have missionary barrels, 'cause he isn't a minister like—well, you know." Her face reddened. "She wears real pretty clothes sometimes in spite of being poor. Aunt Polly, what's a divorce? She said if they got it, they wouldn't live here anymore."

"They aren't going away, dear. They're going to stay right here together and play the game, the way you wanted. She said it would make you glad to know."

Pollyanna quickly looked up. "Why, Aunt Polly, do *you* know about the game? You sound as if you do."

"Yes, and it's beautiful, and I'm going to play it."

"Oh, *Aunt Polly*, you? I'm so glad! I've wanted you to play it most of anybody, all this time."

Aunt Polly caught her breath. "I think the whole town is playing, even the minister. I met Mr. Ford in the village this morning, and he said as soon as you can see him, he's coming to tell you that he hasn't stopped being glad over those eight-hundred rejoicing texts. All the world is wonderfully happier because of one little girl who taught people a new game and how to play it."

Pollyanna clapped her hands. "Why, there *is* something I can be glad about, after all. I can be glad I've *had* my legs, else I couldn't have done—that!"

The short winter days came and went but they were not short to Pollyanna, but long and sometimes filled with pain. She prayed a lot and asked her Heavenly Father to help her play the game, now that Aunt Polly was playing it so well. Her aunt brought home stories: of two waifs who crawled under a blown-down door in a snowstorm

SHE ASKED HER HEAVENLY FATHER TO HELP HER PLAY THE GAME

and wondered what poor folks did if they didn't have any door! And the poor old lady who only had two teeth but was so glad those two teeth "hit" so she could eat.

Now and then Pollyanna was allowed to have a visitor: John Pendleton once, and Jimmy Bean twice, who told what a first-rate home and bang-up "folks" Mr. Pendleton made. But when spring came and Pollyanna didn't improve, Dr. Chilton called on John Pendleton one Saturday morning. Jimmy Bean, weeding in the flowerbed beneath the open window, opened his ears wide and heard everything they said.

"Pendleton, I want to see that child. I *must* make an examination, but I can't. You, of all people in town, know I haven't been inside the Harrington door for fifteen years. The mistress of the house told me the next time she asked me to enter I might take it she was begging my pardon, that all was as before—which meant she'd marry me. She won't summon me."

"Couldn't you go without a summons?"

"I MUST MAKE AN EXAMINATION"

"Hardly. I have pride, too; not the kind that forgets a quarrel, but professional pride. I can't just butt in on other doctors and say, 'Here I am,' can I?"

"Chilton, what was the quarrel?" John Pendleton asked.

"Who knows? A silly wrangle, maybe over the size of the moon or the depth of the river. Nothing compared with the years of misery that have followed, but never mind. I must see that child. It may mean life or death. It will mean—I honestly believe—nine chances out of ten, that Pollyanna Whittier will walk again!"

Jimmy Bean sat up with a jerk, eyes wide, when Dr. Chilton went on. "Her case is much like one a college friend of mine helped—he's been studying such for years—but I must *see* Pollyanna to be sure. Dr. Warren has been decent; he told me he suggested consulting with me at the very first, but Miss Harrington said 'no' so decidedly he didn't dare bring it up again. How can I see Pollyanna without a direct request from her aunt? She's too proud and angry to ask me, even after all these years."

"IT MAY MEAN LIFE OR DEATH"

"If she could be made to see and understand—"

"Yes, but who's going to do it?" Dr. Chilton groaned.

Outside the window, Jimmy Bean whispered exultantly, "Well, by Jinks. *I'm* a-goin' to do it!" He rose, crept stealthily around the corner of the house and ran with all his might down Pendleton Hill, straight to the Harrington house and knocked.

"Jimmy Bean wants to see you, ma'am," Nancy announced to Miss Polly.

"Are you sure he didn't mean Pollyanna? He may see her for a few minutes today, if he likes."

"I told him, but he said 'twas you he wanted."

Puzzled and surprised, Miss Polly found a round-eyed, flushed-face boy who began to speak at once.

"I s'pose what I'm doin' an' sayin' is dreadful, but I'd walk over hot coals for Pollyanna or face you or anythin' like that. An' I think you would, too, if you thought there was a chance for her to walk again. So I come to tell ye that as long as it's only pride that's keepin' Pollyanna from

"I S'POSE WHAT I'M DOIN' AN' SAYIN' IS DREADFUL..."

walkin', why I knew you *would* ask Dr. Chilton here—"

"Wh-at?" Miss Polly's look of stupefaction changed to anger.

"I didn't mean to make ye mad. I just heard Dr. Chilton an' Mr. Pendleton talkin' in the library—'twasn't sneak listenin'; I was weedin'. Dr. Chilton knows some doctor that can cure Pollyanna, he thinks, but he told Mr. Pendleton ye wouldn't let him come. He can't on account of pride an' professional somethin', but they didn't know who could make ye understand, and I says to myself, 'By Jinks, I'll do it!' An' I come—and have I made ye understand?"

"Yes," Aunt Polly feverishly said. "Who's the doctor, and are they *sure* he could make Pollyanna walk?"

"He's just cured somebody just like her. Say, you will let Dr. Chilton come, won't you?"

After a minute she said brokenly, "Yes. Now run home, Jimmy—quick! I've got to speak to Dr. Warren, who's upstairs."

A little later Dr. Warren met an agitated, flushed-face

"I'VE GOT TO SPEAK TO DR. WARREN"

Miss Polly in the hall and was surprised when she said, "I once refused to let Dr. Chilton come in for a consultation. I have reconsidered. I very much desire you to call him in. Will you not ask him at once—please?"

Dr. Warren and a tall, broad-shouldered man soon entered Pollyanna's room where the prisms made dancing rainbows on the ceiling. "Dr. Chilton, I am so glad to see you!" she said joyously. "But if Aunt Polly doesn't want—"

"It's all right, dear." Her aunt hurried forward. "He's going to look you over with Dr. Warren this morning. I asked him to come. That is—"

The adoring happiness in Dr. Chilton's face sent her scurrying from the room, cheeks pink. The doctor held out both hands to Pollyanna. "Little girl, one of the gladdest jobs you ever did has been done today," he said in a shaken voice.

At twilight, a tremulous, wonderfully different Aunt Polly crept to Pollyanna's bedside. "Pollyanna, dear, I'm

" I ASKED HIM TO COME "

going to tell you first of all. Someday, I'm going to give you Dr. Chilton for your—uncle. You did it, Pollyanna, and I'm so happy—and so glad, darling!"

Pollyanna clapped then stopped. "Aunt Polly, *you* were the woman's heart and hand he wanted so long ago. I know! I'm so glad, I don't mind even my legs so much now."

"Perhaps someday, dear—" Aunt Polly did not finish. She didn't dare tell the hope that Dr. Chilton had put into her heart. She did say, "Next week, you're going to take a journey on a nice, comfortable bed and in cars and carriages to a great doctor who has a big house miles away made on purpose for just such people as you. He's a dear friend of Dr. Chilton's, and we're going to see what he can do for you!"

The letter from the sanitorium many miles away and many months later hit Beldingsville like a shower of heavenly blessings; and like puddles from a summer storm, the

"WE'RE GOING TO SEE WHAT HE CAN DO FOR YOU!"

news spread to the dozens of friends who had waited and prayed and continued to play the glad game since Pollyanna left Vermont.

"Dear Aunt Polly and Uncle Tom and Nancy,—Oh, I can—I can—*I can* walk! I did it today all the way from my bed to my window! It was six steps. My, how good it was to be on legs again.

"All the doctors stood around and smiled, and all the nurses stood beside them and cried. A lady in the next ward who walked last week first, peeked in, and another, who hopes she can walk next month, was invited in to the party, and she lay on my nurse's bed and clapped her hands. Even Black Tilly who washes the floor, looked through the piazza window and called me 'Honey child' when she wasn't crying too much to call me anything.

"I don't see why they cried. I wanted to sing and shout and yell. Just think, *I can walk*. Now, I don't mind being here almost ten months, and I didn't miss the wedding, anyhow. Wasn't that just like you, Aunt Polly, to come on

"'OH, I CAN- I CAN- I CAN WALK!'"

here and get married right beside my bed, so I could see you. You always do think of the gladdest things!

"Pretty soon, they say, I shall go home. I wish I could walk all the way there, I do. I don't think I shall ever want to ride anywhere any more. It will be so good just to walk. Oh, I'm so glad! I told God that I am even glad now I lost my legs for awhile, for you never, never know how perfectly lovely legs are till you haven't got them—legs that go, I mean. I'm going to walk eight steps tomorrow.

With heaps of love to everybody,

Pollyanna

'The Glad Girl'"

THE GLAD GIRL !

AWESOME BOOKS FOR KIDS!

The Young Reader's Christian Library
Action, Adventure, and Fun Reading!

This series for young readers ages 8 to 12 is action-packed, fast-paced, and Christ-centered! With exciting illustrations on every other page following the text, kids won't be able to put these books down! Over 100 illustrations per book. All books are paperbound. The unique size (4 3/16" x 5 3/8") makes these books easy to take anywhere!

A Great Selection to Satisfy All Kids!

Abraham Lincoln	*In His Steps*	*Prudence of Plymouth*
Ben-Hur	*Jesus*	*Plantation*
Billy Sunday	*Joseph*	*Robinson Crusoe*
Christopher Columbus	*Lydia*	*Roger Williams*
Corrie ten Boom	*Miriam*	*Ruth*
David Livingstone	*Paul*	*Samuel Morris*
Deborah	*Peter*	*The Swiss Family*
Elijah	*The Pilgrim's Progress*	*Robinson*
Esther	*Pocahontas*	*Taming the Land*
Heidi	*Pollyanna*	*Thunder in the Valley*
Hudson Taylor		*Wagons West*